PADDINGTON'S GARDEN

Paddington Picture Book 2

For older children Michael Bond has
written nine Paddington story books,
all illustrated by Peggy Fortnum

Text © Copyright Michael Bond 1972
Illustrations © Copyright Fred Banbery 1972

First published August 1972
Sixth reprint 1976

ISBN 0 00 182113 X

Printed in Great Britain
Collins Clear-Type Press, London and Glasgow

Paddington's Garden

by

MICHAEL BOND AND

illustrated by

FRED BANBERY

COLLINS

ST JAMES'S PLACE, LONDON

One day Paddington decided to make a list of all
the nice things there were about being a bear
and living with the Browns at number thirty-two
Windsor Gardens.

It was a long list and he had almost reached the
end of the paper when he suddenly realized
he'd left out one of the nicest things of all . . .
the garden itself!

Paddington liked the Browns' garden. It was
quiet and peaceful, and there were times when it
might not have been in London at all.

But nice gardens usually mean a lot of hard work,
and after a day at his office Mr Brown often
wished it wasn't quite so large.

It was Mrs Brown who first thought of giving
Jonathan, Judy and Paddington a piece each of
their own.

"It will keep them out of mischief," she said.

"And it will help you at the same time."

So Mr Brown marked out three squares, and to make it more exciting he said he would give a prize to whoever had the best idea.

Early next morning all three set to work.
Judy thought she would grow some flowers,
and Jonathan started to make a paved garden,
but Paddington didn't know what to do.

Gardening was much harder than it looked –
especially with paws, and he soon grew tired of
digging.

In the end he decided to do some shopping.
He had some savings left over from his pocket
money and he bought a wheelbarrow, a trowel,

and a large packet of assorted seeds.

It seemed very good value indeed – especially as he still had two pence left over.

The shopkeeper told him that when planning a new garden it was a good idea to stand some way away first in order to picture what it would look like when it was finished. So, taking a jar of his best chunky marmalade, Paddington set out to visit the nearby building site.

By the time he got there it was the middle of the
morning, and as the men were all at their tea
break he sat down on a pile of bricks, put the

jar of marmalade on a wooden platform for
safety, and then peered hopefully towards the
Browns' garden.

After sitting there for some while without getting
a single idea Paddington decided to try taking a
short walk instead.

When he got back his eyes nearly popped out.
A man was emptying the concrete mixer on
the very spot where he'd left his jar of chunky
marmalade!

At that moment the foreman came round the
corner and seeing the look on Paddington's face
he stopped to ask what was wrong.

Paddington pointed to the pile of wet cement.
"All my chunks have been buried!" he
exclaimed hotly.

The foreman called his men together. "There's a young bear gentleman here who's lost some very valuable chunks," he said urgently.

They set to work clearing the cement.

Soon the ground was covered with small piles, but still there was no sign of Paddington's jar.

Suddenly there was a whirring sound from somewhere overhead and to Paddington's surprise a platform landed at his feet.

"My marmalade!" he exclaimed thankfully.

"Your marmalade?" echoed the foreman, staring at the jar. "Did you say *marmalade*?"

"That's right," said Paddington. "I put it there ready for my tea break. It must have been taken up by mistake."

It was the foreman's turn to look as if he could
hardly believe his eyes.

"That's special quick-drying cement!" he
wailed. "It's probably going rock-hard already—

ruined by a bear's marmalade! No one will give me two pence for it now!"

Paddington opened his suitcase and felt in the secret compartment. "I will," he said eagerly.

Paddington took the lumps of concrete home in
his wheelbarrow and worked hard in his garden
for the rest of the day. When the builders saw
the rockery he had made with the concrete they
were most impressed and gave Paddington
several plants to finish it off for the time being...

. . . until his seeds started to grow.

Paddington's rockery fitted in so well with
Jonathan's paved garden and Judy's flower bed
it looked as though the whole thing had been
planned.

Mr Brown was so pleased he decided to give
them all an extra week's pocket money, and that
evening they celebrated by having tea in the
new garden.

After it was over Paddington stayed on for a while in order to finish off his list of all the nice things there were about being a bear and living at number thirty-two Windsor Gardens.

He had one more important item to add.

MY ROCKERY

Then he signed his name and added his special paw print . . .

. . . just to show it was genuine.